Chilly Knob

Map

PAPA'S ANGELS

A CHRISTMAS STORY

COLLIN WILCOX PAXTON & GARY CARDEN

NEW WORLD LIBRARY
NOVATO, CALIFORNIA

New World Library
14 Pamaron Way
Novato, California 94949

© 1996 Collin Wilcox Paxton
Based on the play by Collin Wilcox Paxton
Cover design: Nita Ybarra
Illustrations: Elsa Sibley
Music: John Roman
Text design: Aaron Kenedi

Library of Congress Cataloging-in-Publication Data

Wilcox Paxton, Collin, 1935–
Papa's angels : a Christmas story / Collin Wilcox Paxton
& Gary Carden

p.   cm

ISBN 1-57731-004-7 (alk. paper)

[1. Fathers--Fiction. 2. Christmas--Fiction. 3. Grief--Fiction
4. Death--Fiction.]   I. Carden, Gary, 1935– . II. Title
PZ7.W645715Pap 1996   96-24238
[Fic]--dc20   CIP
                                                          AC

First printing, October 1996
Printed in the U.S.A. on acid-free paper
Distributed to the trade by Publishers Group West

10 9 8 7 6 5 4 3 2 1

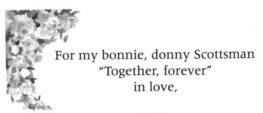

For my bonnie, donny Scottsman
"Together, forever"
in love,

Collin

For Ada Burnette Passmore, wherever you are;
And for Sara Louise, who is up on the hill.

Gary Carden

And for

Chelsea,
Caleb,
and
Hannah

♥
j

THIS IS WHAT HAPPENED SINCE MOMMA DIED. It's been two weeks today since it happened. John Neal asked me if we could go visit Momma, so after Papa left and the chores was all done, John Neal told Hannah Rose and Alvin where we were going, since they were sorta in charge until we got back. Maude was playing by herself, so we set out. John Neal's jest five, and so it took a while. He's too big to carry, so we had to walk slow, down Billy's Cabin Road and way across Walking Stick Hill. It was windy and the leaves was falling like orange and yellow snow.

John Neal played all the way. He would dive into them big piles of leaves and hide. He had Fuzzy peeping out from his overall bib. Fuzzy is this rabbit skin with two buttons Momma sewed on it for eyes, and one for its nose. John Neal takes it everwheres. Oh, they had fun! John Neal talks to Fuzzy, but I don't know what he says. He whispers real low and sometimes he laughs like Fuzzy said something funny.

Afore we stopped going to Balm of Gilead Baptist Church, Papa and Momma, Hannah Rose, Maude, Alvin, John Neal and me would all go to Sunday School. Sometimes, Miz Scruggs, our Sunday School teacher, would try to take Fuzzy away from John Neal 'cause she said it was not right for a child to talk to a rabbit skin. John Neal would hold on to Fuzzy, though. She tried to talk to Papa and Momma 'bout it, and Papa told Miz Scruggs to mind her own business. Then, after Momma died and Hannah Rose took to wearing overalls and pants like a boy, Miz Scruggs forgot all about Fuzzy. She was so upset by Hannah Rose that she talked to our Sunday School Class. That was the last time we went to church.

When we got to the graveyard, Momma's grave was covered with red and yellow leaves. There was a big wreath still there. It had red and white flowers that was beginning to fade, and a big green ribbon that said, "Gone Before." The little marker that Papa had made had fell over, so I stood it up. It said, "Sharon Jenkins, 1902 –1935" and down under that, "Goodbye Sun." Papa had carved all the letters and numbers with his pocket knife.

When Preacher Polk asked Papa about the words, Papa said that was the way he felt, that the sun had gone out of his life. The preacher said, "Brother Jenkins, where is God? Does your grief not have room for God and hope?" Papa jest stared at him. Then, he said, "Where was God and hope for Sharon?" That was the beginning, I guess. Papa was closing doors and boarding up windows. He was saying Goodbye Sun.

I started to sweep the leaves from Momma's grave with my hands, but John Neal said, "Becca, leave them be." Then, he gathered more leaves in his arms and carried them to the grave. In a little while, he had a huge pile. Then, he did the strangest thing. He crawled inside them leaves! After a while, I could hear him whispering, his little voice sounding like mice in the attic. Well, I thought, what would Miz Scruggs make of this!

On the way home, John Neal told me that him and Fuzzy had talked to Momma.

I looked at John Neal real hard.

"Honest Injun," he said, looking all solemn and serious.

"She said that we should make Papa laugh."

Then, he was gone, jumping into the places

where the leaves had drifted, and running through the woods along the trail.

Make Papa laugh. Easier said than done! To look at him now, you'd never guess that Papa's nickname is "Grins." That's what his friends alwus called him, "Grins" Jenkins. Used to be, he was alwus cutting up, making jokes, playing that funny old guitar that he's got. Grammy says that he was alwus jest a fun-box as far back as she could remember. But no more. After Momma died, Papa put his guitar up on a shelf in the bedroom closet, and he ain't made music since. "No more music," he said. I don't like to think 'bout Papa and the guitar much, 'cause it makes me feel so sad. Maybe I'll write more 'bout it later.

T HIS IS ABOUT WHERE WE LIVE AND SCHOOL.
There is five of us children and Papa. We live
in a cabin that Papa built. It has five rooms and an
attic. John Neal is five, and he sleeps with Alvin,
who is nine, in the attic. Hannah Rose is ten and
she sleeps with Maude, who is seven. I am the
oldest, almost thirteen, and I have a room all to
myself, and that is good! We all go to the Wide
Awake Elementary, which is real close to home.
Before Momma died, we used to come out on the
playground at recess and we could see Momma

on our porch, and she would wave.

Now, when we look at the house, the porch is empty. Papa don't wave. He don't even come out on the porch.

The Wide Awake Elementary is grades lst through 8th, and we are all there except John Neal, who is at home. There are sixty-three students in the school, and some of the grades are in the same room. Like Alvin is in the 4th grade and Hannah Rose is in the 5th and they are in the same room. The 5th is on the left and the 4th on the right with a big aisle in the middle. I'm in the 7th and smart for my age. Maude is in the 2nd grade.

John Neal and Me

Momma

THIS IS ABOUT HOW MOMMA DIED. It was consumption. That is what the doctor called it. Momma had always had a little cough and sometimes she jest give out and had to rest, but when she coughed up blood, Papa got the doctor. I guess the big shock was when the Doctor said that we might get it, too. He said doctors didn't know a lot about the consumption, but until they did, it was best to "isolate" the sick person. He told Papa that Momma could go off to the sanitarium where she would be took care of, and Papa said no, he would take care of her. He said he'd seen the sanitarium over at Bug Hill, and that he remembered the little open-air rooms that looked like tents, and the sick people looking so lonely, sittin' in their rooms.

The doctor said that it was foolish to "endanger" the lives of the rest of the family. Papa said he could do everything for Momma that a doctor could and we wouldn't "endanger" anybody's life. The doctor said that cleanliness was the most important thing, and that every object that Momma touched had to be scalded in hot water and the room cleaned every day. So, Papa built Momma a special room.

It was sorta added on to the bedroom, but Papa fixed it so that the sun was always shining into Momma's room. There was a big glass window so we could see Momma and she could see us. Papa is such a good carpenter, he fixed it real nice, and we would all set together in the evening, Momma in her room and us on the porch. Papa would slide her food on a little tray through a little opening in the wall. At first, it was strange with Momma being so close and yet so far away. She talked and laughed like alwus, but sometimes I would see a look on her face, so sad, and then I would see Papa looking at her. Momma would change her own bed and Papa would put fresh wildwood flowers in a big bowl on her night table. In the afternoon, Momma would stand in the sun, when it moved across the floor she would move with it. It was like she wanted to soak up the last little ray of the sun, like she was thirsty for sunshine like other people might be thirsty for water.

Sometimes, there was blood on Momma's pillow, or the bed sheet. The doctor said that anything with blood on it had to be burned. Papa did that. Hannah Rose and me boiled water ever'day and Papa would clean Momma's room while she set in her chair close to the window with the sun on her face.

Sometimes, Papa would sing to Momma. A long

time ago, he had made up a special song for her. It was called "The Maple Tree Song," and Papa said it was a courtin' song. Momma told us that when she and Papa begun courtin' they used to set under a ole maple tree out in Grammy's yard. Papa had to go overseas during the war, and afore he left he made up this song for Momma and he sung it to her. It was real close to Christmas when he went away and he was gone for three years. Momma used to sing the song when she was lonesome.

Red, gold and yellow leaves,
*   all fall on me;*
Blanket of memories,
*   Old maple tree.*
Summer has gone away,
*   all fall on me;*
Winter is calling you,
*   Old maple tree.*
Winter is calling,

so stoke up the fire;
Deep in the night
   may you warm us a while.
Christmas is coming,
   so stoke up the fire;
Spirit of love,
   may you warm us a while.

Springtime will come,
   but while we are apart,
I'll fold your memory
   into my heart.

Love, if you miss me
   while we are apart,
I'll send you a sign of love
   into your heart.

One morning, she couldn't get up. After that she would sit propped up in the bed and talk to us through the window. Neighbors would come sometimes and set with us and they would talk long into the night. Sometimes, Papa would get his guitar and there would be singing. Papa hated to be separated from Momma and he talked more and more about the foolishness of talking to his wife through a glass window. Towards the last, Momma laid there looking like the faded wildflowers in the bowl by her bed. Her voice got to be a whisper and the coughing hurt her. That is when Papa said to hell with it and went into her room. He cared for her, slept on the floor, set by the bed. People stopped coming to visit. The music stopped, too.

Papa made the coffin. It was red cherry, and it was the prettiest thing he ever made. I seen him put Momma in it. The doctor had left after saying a lot of things about "the wisdom of a quick burial" which upset Papa. He took the quilt that Grammy had given them on their wedding day, all yellow and red and blue, and he wrapped Momma in it and carried her to the coffin. He put Momma in, and then he set the coffin on two chairs in front of the big window in Momma's room. We set and watched the sun glitter on the coffin, and Momma's face poking up out of that quilt like a pale flower that had bloomed in the sunshine.

I went in Momma's room afore she died and she talked to me.

Sometime, I'll write 'bout that.

THIS IS WHAT HAPPENED WITH PAPA AT THE SCHOOL. The trouble started when Hannah Rose beat up Ludlow Wacky at recess. She jest didn't beat him up. She run him all the way home. His daddy brung him back to school and told the principal that Ludlow was afraid to come back by hisself. Ludlow thought Hannah Rose was waiting for him, and that she would jump out of the bushes and beat him up again. Mister Wacky was real upset and said he wondered what the world was coming to when abody was afraid to come to school because he might be attacked by "a white-trash Jezebel." What was getting left out of the story was what Ludlow had been doing to Alvin.

First, Alvin come home with a big bruise on his forehead, and said he fell off the seesaw. Then, he come home with a bloody nose and said he got hit by a baseball. Then, he had a black eye. The next day, Hannah Rose watched to see where Alvin went at recess. When he didn't come out on the playground, she went looking for him. He was in the boy's bathroom and Ludlow Wacky was yelling at him from the hall where the whole fifth grade was waiting to see what would happen.

Ludlow was making fun of Alvin's stutter, which he only gets when he gets excited or upset. "Co-co-come out, Sc-sc-scaredy-ca-ca-cat," he yelled. Ludlow weighs about 200 pounds and looks a lot like a pig.

I was on my way to the library, and Lilly Delphia Evitt told me in the hall that "something was happening to Alvin down at the restrooms." I got there jest before Hannah Rose hit Ludlow.

It was a pretty good lick. Ludlow went down like a sack of salt. The hall kinda shook when he hit. It was a strange sight to see Hannah Rose dancing around Ludlow. I guess she might weigh 75 pounds, and she was acting real strange. "Git up, hog face," she said. She was talking out of the side of her mouth. She had on a pair of Alvin's overalls and this porkpie cap that Papa used to wear when he played music and which she had took to wearing after Momma died. Ludlow's nose was bleeding some.

Ludlow run into the boy's bathroom. I guess he thought he would be safe in there. Hannah Rose jest went in after him. Then, Ludlow screamed, and then he come out with Hannah Rose on him like a chicken on a June bug. We heard the hall doors slam behind them and by the time we got outside, we could see Ludlow hitting the high spots down the trail with Hannah Rose still all over him. She come back alone and went in the building. In a minute or two, here come Hannah Rose out with Alvin.

The whole story come out in the principal's office. Ludlow had been picking on Alvin for weeks, ever since Alvin had started stuttering, which was after Momma died. Alvin didn't seem all that happy 'bout Hannah Rose whupping Ludlow. "I'd jest as soon not git saved by my sister," he said. He had a real hard time with the words saved and soon and sister. Hannah Rose said that somebody had to look after the family, and if she had to, she would whup Ludlow again tomorrow. Mr. Wacky, who was jest a bigger Ludlow, said that no dangerous heathen was going to harm his son, and then, Papa was there!

Where did he come from? How did he know to come, anyway? His hair was messed up and his shirttail was out. He was out of breath, too, like he had been running.

First off, Papa asked Mister Wacky if he wanted to step outside and repeat what he had said about Hannah Rose. Mister Wacky said he didn't want to step outside, and civilized people didn't settle their differences with violence, and Hannah Rose, talking mean out of the side of her mouth, said, yeah, tell that to Ludlow. The principal said some stuff about talking later when ever'body had cooler heads. Mr. Wacky left talking about seeing a lawyer, and Ludlow went back to his 5th grade class and Hannah Rose said, "Oink, Oink" when he went out the door. Papa and Alvin and Hannah Rose and me stayed 'cause the principal said he needed to talk to "the Jenkins family."

The principal, who had come all the way from Raleigh to be the principal of Wide Awake School, told Papa that he was concerned about Alvin and Hannah Rose. He said that he was touched by our recent "be-rave-ment," and that the loss of a loved one brought changes. But, he said that he thought that our changes was "highly unusual." He said some things about Alvin's "speech im-ped-i-mint," and the fact that Hannah Rose had took to acting like a boy. He said that he was concerned that she had "brut-a-lized" the son of a "prom-in-ent" businessman, and that she had gone too far. Papa said that as near as he could tell, Hannah Rose had jest done what somebody else should have done long ago, and then he give Alvin a real hard look. Papa went over and stood real close to the principal and said that he might not be a "prom-in-ent" businessman, but he wasn't going to let his children be run over by "high mucky mucks." The principal said that he didn't think alcohol solved problems, and Papa said he didn't think so either, and what did that have to do with anything, anyways. He was getting madder by the minute, and his face was getting red. The principal sniffed like he smelled something bad and said some things about "conditions." He said Alvin could remain in school "on condition" that Papa agreed to send him to this speech doctor, and that Hannah Rose would have to wear "acceptable clothes." I guess he meant dresses. One thing led to another and Papa told him he could go to hell, and then we all went home.

THIS IS WHAT I FOUND OUT ABOUT PAPA. I'll start with what happened yesterday when we got home from Wide Awake. I guess we was a pretty sad bunch by the time we started up Billy's Cabin Road 'cause nobody was talking. Little John Neal and Maude was watching for us. I guess they had been real worried. John Neal waved through the window and I seen him tell Fuzzy that we was home. I thought it was a good thing that John Neal was not old enough to go to school 'cause he would have been in the principal's office with Fuzzy while the principal was talking 'bout how strange the Jenkins family was getting. I guess maybe Maude was the only one that was normal. And maybe me. Well, I'm almost normal. Then, it come to me that Maude was the one that told Papa what was happening at school. She run all the way home and got him.

Sure enough, as soon as we got in the house, Maude told me that when the trouble started, she went to git Papa. I guess I looked puzzled, 'cause she said that she knew where to find him. He wasn't out looking for work like he said. He was out in the barn where he alwus was. I didn't know that. Maude said he was jest setting in the dark in the feed-room. I wondered why he was out there in that empty barn. Well, almost empty. Our horse, Joe, is gone now. There's jest Ellie May, the cow left. After the big drought this fall, Papa said we couldn't afford to keep Joe. I sure miss him a whole lot.

Then, Papa made a speech. He said he didn't

want Hannah Rose bothering Ludlow, and Hannah Rose said that didn't seem likely since she wouldn't be going back to school, which she said she was glad of, and why was Papa talking like that now when he had took up for her at school. Papa said that families stuck together when there was trouble, but that didn't mean that he "approved of" what she had done. Then, he asked Alvin why he hadn't whupped Ludlow hisself. Alvin jest got real quiet. Then, Papa talked about how we had to take care of each other, and that each of us had our chores to do and wasn't it suppertime?

Then, me and Hannah Rose pretended to cook. We have been pretending for a long time. We even tried to cook "for real" for a while, but nobody could eat it. We had to bury Hannah Rose's biscuits out behind the barn. The biscuits and the stack cake. But, then Hannah Rose told Grammy, and she told us not to worry, that she would cook for us. Hannah Rose said, but Papa won't let you come in the house, and Grammy said she would bring the food when Papa wasn't at home. So ever' morning, Grammy watched until she seen Papa leave the house, and then she would bring all this good stuff. Biscuits, and corn-bread and chicken, and green beans and even a stack cake ever' now and then. Then, we would pretend to cook supper and breakfast. All we done was build a fire in the stove and warm stuff up. I can make coffee, and Papa, he never knew the difference! Grammy said that he wouldn't notice. She said Papa couldn't see nothing but his own misery.

After supper, when Papa went to sleep in the big chair in front of the fireplace, I lit the lantern and went out to the barn. Sure enough, there was a chair in the feed-room in front of a shelf. Momma's picture was on the shelf, beside her dulcimore. There wasn't a window, and I couldn't see no sign that Papa had been working on anything. Besides farming, Papa is a carpenter and he makes chairs and pie-safes and tables. But there wasn't anything there. I thought that was strange. Did Papa jest come out here and set in the dark? Then, I seen the little kerosene lamp. It was setting on the shelf by Momma's picture. I could even read what Papa had wrote on the picture, "My Rose of Sharon, My Angel." It was a wedding picture.

Then, I seen something else. A bullet. It was setting there on the shelf by Momma's picture. What was it doing there? It was brass, and it sorta glowed in the lantern-light. I looked around a little, and I found the gun. It was wrapped in an oily rag in the cotton-seed barrel.

What did it all mean?

Well, I sure did have a lot to think about! Did Papa come out here ever day after he pretended to go off looking for work and set here looking at Momma's picture? What about the bullet and gun? I felt like a cold winter wind had blowed through my clothes and chilled my heart. I decided not to think about the gun and bullet. I decided not to show anybody what I had found either.

THIS IS ABOUT MY BOOK. Whoever is reading this, maybe you have noticed something about what I have been writing. It's about me and that I never tell you what I had to say to Papa or John Neal or Grammy or anybody. That is because I can't talk.

Momma told me that when I was a baby, she and Papa got worried when I never said anything, so they took me to a big clinic in Asheville, and they took all kind of tests. They said that I would never talk. When I started school, the teachers was real nice, and I guess I got used to writing what I had to say. Hannah Rose, Alvin, Maude, and John Neal, they are all used to me not talking, and they never leave me out of things.

When I had questions, I wrote notes. I used to save them up in my pocket, and I would give them to Momma or Grammy. Things like "What is the name of the color on the edge of Chilly Knob that comes jest before the sun shuts its eye?" or "If sounds were colors, what color is the rooster's crow?" or "What does the kettle sing about?"

When Momma was real sick, she called me and I went in her bedroom alone. We never, never did that, but when the Doctor and Papa both said it was alright "for a minute or two," I knew Momma was saying goodbye. We went in, one at a time.

She said, "I wanted to talk to you alone, Becca. If

the others were here, it might hurt them to hear what I want to say." She patted the bed, and I crawled up beside her. Then, she whispered to me, "You are a very special little girl, Becca. Maybe it is because you can't talk, you have been given a special gift. You can say things with writin' that most of us can't say when we talk." Then she slipped her thin hand under the bed pillow and come out with a little book. It had a lavender cloth cover and all the pages inside it was blank. Momma had cross-stitched pink and white Simplicity Roses around the cover of the book. Momma jest loved roses. They was so real looking you felt like you wanted to smell them. I wondered, when I looked at her pretty stitching, when she done it.

Momma smiled at me and said, "Promise me that you will do something special with your gift."

And I promised Momma that I would.

Grammy put it different. She said when you lost

something like seeing, feeling or hearing, you was given "something else." "Because you cannot speak with a voice, you have been given the gift of writin' what your heart says."

Miss Calloway at school told me 'bout "signing," an' I use it some to talk to her and the other children. I have a book she ordered for me, too, but I make up lots of the signs. My friends know what I mean, so it's alright.

So now, you know. This is my book, and it tells you what I cannot say any other way.

THIS IS WHAT HAPPENED BETWEEN PAPA AND GRAMMY. Grammy lives on the ridge behind our house and she is my very favorite person in all the world. She is Papa's Momma and everbody, 'cept us, calls her Grandma Dory. Alvin and Hannah Rose and me, we used to go see Grammy everday. It's like a magic world up on Chilly Knob. There is a spotted pony named Satulah that is never locked up and sometimes he puts his head through the open window in Grammy's kitchen where we feed him sugar cubes. There is a deaf white cat named Spook that lives in the house and plays with shadows on the floor. In the summer, there are calla lilies and ducks and tame rabbits. Animals love Grammy, and they know that nothing will hurt them at her house. The huge ole maple tree that Momma and Papa courted under 'bout covers the front yard, and in the summer, the cabbages in Grammy's garden are big as pumpkins and the tomatoes are as big as cabbages! Like John Neal said once, "Everthing is bigger and better at Grammy's!"

Grammy understood how much I missed our horse, Joe, after Papa said we couldn't afford him no more. To me he was the same as people. Joe was my friend, and I loved him. Grammy calls all animals "our kindred spirits," even wild ones. She says ever critter has a special lesson to teach folks, if folks would jest pay attention. We used to go out by ourselves, way deep in the woods back of Chilly Knob. We'd set out there as still as two stones. Soon, here would come the critters. If a shy little deer was to come by she'd say it teaches gentleness. Or if a mouse peeked out of its hole she'd say it taught us about looking at things real close. She told that owl feathers is silent and you can never hear a owl fly. And she said that foxes showed us how not to be seen if we didn't want to be. I don't know how she knows all them things that she knows.

Grammy is supposed to have "second sight." Momma used to say that she sensed things 'fore they happened, and I guess it must be so. Like, she made baby clothes for Blicka Dee Picklesimer's twins, and she brung them to Blicka Dee before the twins was born. And she made a burying quilt for her own mother, Granny Pop. Took her two months to make it and she finished it the night that Granny Pop died. She knows when folks is sick and she cooks a meal and bakes a cake for company that ain't even got to her house yet.

Papa says he don't put no truck in such foolishness. He asked Grammy why she didn't know about Momma before she got sick. Grammy said that was the way it was sometimes. Said it was like picking up radio stations on a crystal set, and that she might pick up things a good way off, and miss a message that was close by. She said she was jest thankful for what she did pick up.

It jest come to me that we are a lot like Grammy's animals. When we are in Grammy's house, we feel safe. When we set at her old kitchen table watching Spook play with shadows, and Satulah nickering for sugar cubes outside the window, we felt like nothin' could harm us. We could jest set and eat stack cake and smell stuff cooking. Oh, it used to be nice.

But one night after Momma died, when we stayed so late, Papa had to come after us, and things changed. Papa brung John Neal and Maude with him, and John Neal told Grammy about talking to Momma. Papa told John Neal not to talk foolishness and John Neal started to cry and said he missed Momma. Papa got all flustered and said we had better git on down to our house. That's when Grammy said it. She said, "John Neal, your Momma will be home for Christmas." Well, Papa got mad. "Don't be telling a little child foolishness like that," he said. Grammy said it weren't foolish. She said that the people living in these mountains that come here from Scotland and Ireland hundreds of years ago knowed that the dead who was dearly loved come back at Christmas. She said their spirits was in the fireplace, and that when the family gathered around a fire on Christmas, the dead would be there, too.

"Can you see them?" said John Neal.

"No," said Grammy, "not with your eyes. But you can see them with your heart. Some folks even set a place for them at the table."

"That is enough of that!" said Papa, and he herded us out the door into the yard. Then, he went back and said some mean things to

Grammy. We heard ever word he said even though he was in the house with the door closed. He said it was a terrible thing to give children false hope. Grammy said, "Son, I know you think the light has gone out of your life and that it will never return, but you can't go on the way you are going." She said, "Think of the children! Don't you see what your grief is doing to them?"

Papa yelled at her. He said that if she was going to talk foolishness about spirits living in a fireplace, then she wasn't welcome in his home. He said he didn't want his children believing such foolishness. Then, he come out and slammed the door. Grammy come out on the porch and said, "Son, life has to go on. I know that you don't believe it right now, but you will smile again. If you will raise your head and open your heart, it will happen."

Papa carried John Neal and led Maude. Alvin, Hannah Rose and me trooped along behind. When we got home, Papa said we wasn't to go to Grammy's no more. Alvin made a bad mistake,

Hannah Rose on Ludlow

Satulah and Spook

then. He argued with Papa. "Can't we go see her at Ch-Christmas?"

"No," said Papa.

"What k-kind of Ch-Christmas will it be without Grammy?" said Alvin.

"There ain't going to be any Christmas!" shouted Papa.

We was so amazed, we jest gawked at him.

Finally, Alvin said, "What do you mean?"

"I mean jest what I said! I don't want to hear that word mentioned again, you hear?"

"You don't want us to say Ch-Christmas?" said Alvin.

"Or expect it, or even think about it." Papa stared at us, and then, his voice changed, his voice sounded like it had tears in it.

"How could we have Christmas and Sharon

gone? How could we laugh or sing knowing that we will never see her face again? How..." Then, he jest quit talking. He walked out the door into the darkness.

We didn't know what to do. Then, John Neal went to the window and climbed on his stool. He pulled Fuzzy from his overalls bib and whispered to him. Then, he turned and said, "You know what Momma said! She said we must make Papa laugh!"

Alvin sounded jest miserable, and he said, "Might as well make him grow feathers and fly up to the ridge-pole of the house and crow."

Alvin was right, I guess. We didn't seem to be laughing much either. I looked at little John Neal setting alone on that stool, holding onto Fuzzy for dear life, and remembered the night he was born. When Papa and all of us went in the bedroom to see John Neal, there was Fuzzy on the pillow by Momma and John Neal. Momma said that she had made Fuzzy to "grow up" with John Neal. That is when Papa got his guitar, and sung a song to Momma that he said jest come to him. He set on the foot of their bed and sung it, and it was called "Simple Signs of Love."

Should I sing it for the button
sittin' on its fuzzy nose,
Should I sing it for the wonder
as our John Neal up and grows,
Should I sing it mighty thankful, Lord,
for Blessings from Above
I will sing it for these simple signs
of Love ...
Yes, for each and every simple sign
of Love.

You have given us a child, Love,
a blessin' to behold,
You have given me a fam'ly
that I treasure more than gold,

You have given me most ever'thing
  a man could be proud of,
I am singing of your simple signs
  of Love,
Yes, for each and every simple sign
  of Love.

La la la, la la
La la la, la la
La la la, la la la . . .

I am singing of your simple signs
  of Love,
Yes, for each and every simple sign
  of Love.

THIS IS ABOUT PAPA'S GUITAR. Last night, when I wrote about Papa and the way things used to be, it made me sad. When I went to sleep I dreamed about the way things used to be. There was nothing sad 'bout my dreams 'cause I kept waking up happy. In the dream Papa had jest sung a funny song. All night I kept dreaming about Papa's guitar and the family singing. Sometimes, we would be on the porch, or up at Grammy's, or down at the feed barn 'cause Papa played at all them places. He played at dances and parties. Folks was alwus coming to the house to git him to play.

"Come on, Grins," they would say. "There's a square dance at Cashiers Valley, and we need you to play and call!" Papa would go.

He took Momma and all of us with him sometimes, and I was so proud. Me and Momma clapping and all them folks dosy-doing, and Papa hollering out a square-dance call:

> *My true love she's a blue-eyed dandy*
> *Ho-dee-ing-dong-doo-die al-lay day!*

> *A kiss from her is sweeter than candy*
> *Ho-dee-ing-dong-doo-dle al-lay day!*

But most of all, I remember the guitar. Papa said it was magic. He believed in magic then, I guess. It had roses twining around the neck, and there was all these little creatures that was painted around the sound hole that looked like they was crawling in or crawling out of the guitar. There was hummingbirds and redbirds and blue-jays flying around on the back of it. Sometimes, when

Papa picked it up, he would wiggle his eyebrows and say WHOA! And John Neal would say, "What, Papa, what?" Cause that's what he alwus done. Then Papa would say something like, "Oh, there's a good'en in here this time!" And he'd bend over and put his ear down close and listen. Then he would chuckle and laugh jest like John Neal does with Fuzzy, and then, he would say, "We're ready to go!"

Papa said that the guitar almost played itself, and it jest needed him to say its words. He would stop playing sometimes and look flustered and he would ask the guitar, "What? I didn't git that! Tell me again." The guitar would tell him, and he would go on. He said it was like riding a train, and you didn't know where it was going, so the trip was full of surprises. Then, he'd make train sounds and that guitar would start sounding like the little train in Tallulah, Georgia that we saw once when Papa went there to play. Sometimes, Papa would put on his "juice harp" that hung in this wire rack around his neck, and he would make that juice harp huff and chug, and it would start out real slow, going "chug, chugga, chug," and Papa would yell, "Git on board!"

And away we'd go, faster and faster, and then, Whup! the train sounds would stop, and Papa would look jest as surprised as we were, and then he'd sing a song that the guitar give him.

Sometimes, he'd look worried, 'cause he didn't know the next words, and then he'd laugh and nod and go on singing.

The guitar once made a song about me, and Papa sung it. It went:

> *Here comes my sweet Becca!*
> *I would trade a peck-a neck-a*
>   *hugs for one kiss*
> *from my sweet Becca.*

I can't remember no more. It was a silly song, I guess, but it made me feel like somebody had poured cold spring water down the back of my neck. There was songs about ever one of us. A lot of them was 'bout Momma, and she would blush when Papa sung them.

Sometimes, when we was at home and it was jest us having a family singing, Momma would play her dulcimore. Momma never ever played any-wheres but at home. And Papa an' Momma would sing sweet songs together. Then, after, Papa would say, "Call 'em out young'ens. What all you want in this here song?" Then they would all yell out whatever they wanted and Papa and the guitar would make everthing they called out into a song. When the chorus part come around, Papa would give a little nod and ever one joined in. And I sung along in my heart. Oh, we had fun.

But that was before. Papa's guitar is in the closet on the shelf, all wrapped up like it was sick and cold. Maude and me got it down once when Papa was gone. The flowers and the birds and the little animals didn't seem so bright as they used to. It jest seemed like this old guitar. It was out of tune, and when Maude run a finger over the strings, that out-of-tune sound jest hung there in the air like a weak little sunbeam and then it faded. We put it back on the shelf, and wrapped it up in this old quilt. That guitar needed Papa, I thought. The only way it would come alive again is if Papa's hands touches it.

I guess that's the way we all are, too.

THIS IS ABOUT WHEN JIMMY LEE WEBB
COME TO SEE PAPA. We had jest finished
breakfast when Jimmy Lee knocked on the door.
Jimmy Lee goes to school over in Jackson County
and he got a job down at the feed barn in town.
He ain't even sixteen yet, but he acts a lot older.
Jimmy Lee used to make music with Papa, and I
knew soon as I seen him that he was gonna ask
Papa to play somewheres. Sure enough, he did.

"Hey, Grins," he said, grinning and wiggling like

he alwus done, "Let's you and me do a square dance in Cashiers Valley tomorrow night!" He was standing on the porch, laughing and bobbing his head at us. Papa went out on the porch, and Jimmy Lee said:

"They want somebody that knows 'Sourwood Mountain,' an' I done told them that you did!"

"I guess not," Papa said. "I kinda got out of the habit of playing."

"Oh, come on, Grins! You on that guitar an' Gentry on the banjo and me on my fiddle, Whoooo-Wheeee! They be talkin' 'bout us fer the next year!"

Papa smiled. I hadn't seen that in a long time. For a minute, I thought he was gonna do it. Jimmy Lee kept bobbing and grinning, an' I seen him give his little open-handed wave at us through the screen-door. Hannah Rose was standin' next to me at the door and whispered in my ear, "I think Jimmy Lee is sweet on you." I could feel my cheeks gettin' pink as the pinkest Simplicity Rose.

Then Papa said, "No, Jimmy Lee, I don't think I'll be playing no more. I'm sorry you walked all the way up here, but I done told you before that I'm through with all that." Then, he walked off to the barn and left Jimmy Lee standing there.

We felt embarrassed. Jimmy Lee didn't know what to do. He backed off the porch into the yard and jest stood there. Finally, he said, "We miss Grins. We ain't much of a band without him."

He walked down the trail a piece and turned around and said, "If he changes his mind, let me know. I don't mean jest for tomorrow night. I mean if he ever changes his mind. We need him real bad." Then, he waved bye.

"Jimmy Lee, you come back and see Becca, and us too, real soon," said Hannah Rose, jest as bold as you please.

Jimmy Lee's ears got red. "You bet!" he said.

Then he give his little wave and went on down the trail.

We all watched Jimmy Lee walk down Billy's Cabin Road till he was out of sight.

THIS IS ABOUT WHAT GRAMMY TOLD US. I didn't write a thing about Thanksgiving. That is 'cause it come and gone without so much as a fare-thee-well. Oh, there was special food. Leather breeches beans, buttermilk, cracklin corn bread, watermelon pickles, and even a pumpkin pie. Grammy took care of that. But we didn't sing or have a family get-together. The one time we mentioned it, Hannah Rose said, "Hey Papa, it is Thanksgiving!" he give her a look that made her get real quiet. Then, he snorted and said, "What have we got to be thankful 'bout?" I could think of all kinds of things to be thankful 'bout, but from the way Papa said it, I knew that it would be best if nobody said anything. He spent the day staring in the fire, or he would vanish out to the barn. When he come back, I noticed the smell, and I knew what the principal was talking 'bout the day he said that "drinking didn't help."

Papa smells funny. I guess maybe the sour smell had been there a long time and I jest got it confused with the way Papa smelled when he was making things. Turpentine and wood shavings and stuff. But Papa wasn't making furniture.

Thanksgiving morning Grammy brung the food, an' she said, "Well it's time for you young'ens to git a yule log. I don't think we can count on your Papa this year."

"What's that, a yule log?" said Alvin. Seemed like Grammy was talking about something we had never heard of before.

Grammy and Spook

Maude and Alvin

"It's the big oak log that you put in the fireplace on Christmas Eve, and it stays there for the next twelve days," she said.

"Why?" said John Neal.

Grammy was setting on the edge of the porch, and we all come and set around her. Maude got up in her lap. "Come here Becca," said Grammy, "you set next to me." She smelled like apples and cinnamon.

"That's the way you light the 'old fire'," she said, knowing that we would want to know what that was, too. Sure enough, Maude said, "What's the 'old fire'?" Grammy smiled at us an' looked towards the barn. I guess she knew where Papa was. "Come on out here, Hannah Rose. You need to hear this, too." Hannah Rose had been standing in the doorway, listening. She come out and set down by Grammy. "I like that shirt," said Grammy. "Looks better on you than it did on Alvin." Hannah Rose smiled and said, "What's the 'old fire', Grammy?"

"Well, I'll tell you, a long time ago, a long time past, thousands of years I guess, our people used to live in Scotland and Ireland. In the winter when it gits cold, when the days git shorter and the nights git longer, they believed that there come a night when the sun stopped."

"Ah, Grammy," said Alvin. He didn't look like he believed it. "Well, now I didn't say it did stop," said Grammy, "but our people thought it did. It seemed to them that darkness was gitten stronger and light was gitten weaker. It seemed to them that the sun-wheel jest slowed down and stopped, and if they didn't do somethin', it might jest stay that way. The sunshine would fade and the nights would git colder, and it would look like there would never be another spring. The world would jest be cold, bare, and dead."

"What did they do, Grammy?" said John Neal. Him and Fuzzy was hanging on ever word.

"Well, they built fires," said Grammy. "For twelve days, they had fires everwheres. Fires on mountain tops, fires in their homes. They carried torches at night and marched through the dark. See, they thought that if they helped the sun, that the fires they built would give the sun strength. They believed that finally, after twelve days, the sunwheel creaked and moved. Slowly it begun to turn again! When it started, the world was alright for another year. Spring would come, and the flowers would bloom. It happened because they helped the sun. The days would start gitten longer and warmer."

"But, it would happen again, wouldn't it?" said Alvin. "The winter would come back."

"Oh, yes!" said Grammy. "That's how it is. That's the eternal struggle, the one between Light and Dark."

"Who's winning?" said Alvin.

"I guess we are," said Grammy. "We're still here.

But, I git a feeling sometimes that if we stop remembering, if we stop building the fires, bad things could happen."

"Do you believe that the sun stops and we can start it again?" said Alvin.

Grammy thought a while, and then she said, "I believe that people have to become a part of things that change. You endure the cold and dark because you believe that the light and warmth will come back. If you burn a yule log, you are saying that you believe that spring will come again."

"I'll do it then," said Alvin. "I'll git the yule log."

Grammy laughed. "Well, I believe you will!" She caught Alvin's head in the crook of her arm and hugged him, which caused him to git red in the face. "Well, when you do, you come and git me afore you start a fire. There's somethin' else that must be done."

Then, she got up and started home. Half way up Chilly Knob we saw Spook, settin' in the trail waiting. They walked home together, Spook's tail standing straight up like a white pussy willow.

That afternoon, Alvin got the yule log. He found it on the ridge above the house, a huge oak that lightning had struck, and he cut it with Papa's crosscut saw. It took a long time to get it to the house, cause he rolled it. But it's out there now in the middle of the yard. When Papa come in, he looked at it. Then he shrugged and went on in the house. Like Grammy said, he don't seem to see much or question much. Hannah Rose said, "I guess I could paint green and red dots all over my face and quack like a duck and Papa wouldn't notice."

THIS IS ABOUT NOT GOING TO SCHOOL. From the big window, we can see the Wide Awake School. I set with Maude and John Neal and we watch the kids come out at recess. Now, we are seeing the school the way Momma used to see it when she would come out on the porch and wave. Maude and me went out on the porch a couple of times so we could wave at our friends, but they never noticed us standing there. Now, we jest stay in the house and watch.

I miss school. I had friends like Lilly Delphia Evitt

and Retha Jean Whittle. Mostly, the teachers was nice, and I miss English class and Miss Calloway more than I thought I would. School sure looks different from over here. I mean, I can see it all at once, the building and everbody playing, some on seesaws, some playing "Pretty Girl Station" or "Red Rover." When you are at school, you jest see the part you are in. Like, I never noticed Geneva June and Jeter Ward Pickens before. I mean, I seen them all the time, but from over here, I see them different. They are always by theirselves and they stay together and watch the others play, but they don't join in. From over here, I can feel how lonely they are. They wander around, and they will watch the others shoot marbles for a while, and then they will go and stand where the others are lined up facing each other to play "Red Rover." I never noticed before how left out they are. And they look mad, their faces are all stiff. Hannah Rose said that there was something bad had been said 'bout their mother. Why are they left out, I wonder. Is it their fault or do the others leave them out?

Is this the way God sees us? I mean, does he see us like Maude and me see the playground at recess? There goes little Chester Hope and he is off his crutches from breaking his leg in September. And Retha Jean has a new dress. There are Christmas decorations going up in the windows. The bell jest rung and everbody is running back in the building, and Geneva June and Jeter Ward are the last ones in. Why did I never notice how sad they are before?

Now the playground is empty, and I'm thinking we jest keep losing people and things. First Momma, and the drought come and we lost our horse, and then the church, and the school, and now we can't even go to Grammy's and we've lost Satulah and Spook, too. It don't seem right. Now, I'm mad like Geneva June and Jeter Ward Pickens. And I want to go back to school. Hannah Rose and Alvin act like they are glad that they don't have to go, but I don't believe it.

THIS IS ABOUT THE SNOW. It is snowing! These are the biggest flakes I ever seen. John Neal and me walked to Momma's grave in it and it was wonderful. I guess it was six inches deep by the time we got home. It feels so good to be warm and safe when it snows. There we was, all in the house with a cord of wood stacked on the porch, a big fire in the fireplace and plenty of good things in the cook stove's warming closet that Grammy had fixed. Now that is nice! We all set and looked out the window and the snow fell down so thick it looked like feathers from a busted bed tick. John Neal was on his stool so he could see out, and when it got dark, we could see the kerosene lamps at Grammy's house. I liked looking at them glowing through the snow, and knowing that Grammy and Satulah and Spook was up there safe and warm. I could jest see Satulah in his little warm barn chewing hay, and Spook setting in the window washing his foot and looking out at the snow. I guess Grammy was knitting in front of the fire. All of a sudden, I was jest glad to be where I was in our little house on Billy's Cabin Road. Now, if Papa would jest come in, we'd all be together.

THIS IS WHAT HAPPENED AFTER THE SNOW. Well, it is two days after the big snow and some bad things have happened. Last time, I wrote that I wished Papa would come in so we could all be together. Well, he did. But instead of loving the snow, he acted like he hated it. I guess he had been out in the barn all day, and he looked bad. His eyes was red like he had been crying. He asked if the chores was done, and then he asked what that big log was doing out in the middle of the yard.

"That's our yule log," said Alvin.

"Needs splitting," said Papa.

"No," said Alvin, "Grammy said..." I guess he knowed that he had said too much. Papa stared at all of us.

"More foolishness from Grammy," he said. "I told you young'ens not to go up there."

"We didn't, Papa," said Hannah Rose. "We was outside when she come by." That was sorta true. "It's for Christmas," said Maude. Then, she was away and gone, telling Papa about the fire wheel and the "old fire." I tried to catch her eye, but she jest kept going. Papa was getting madder and madder.

"So, we're going to put it in the fireplace on Christmas Eve," she said.

If things wasn't bad enough, little John Neal chimed in with "jest before Santa Claus comes."

Only the way John Neal says it, it sounds like Sandy Claws.

Papa didn't say nothin'. He jest got up an' went over to the fire board and got his pipe. His hands was trembling, and he couldn't find a match to light his pipe anywheres about. Finally, he put the pipe down, and he told us to pay attention.

"I've already told you once that there ain't going to be no Christmas. Now let me tell you why. First, there ain't no money for Christmas, so we can't buy presents."

"But," said Alvin.

"Let me finish," said Papa. "Christmas is a celebration, and we ain't got nothing to celebrate."

Then Alvin stood up to Papa. He said, "Papa, if you don't believe in Christmas an' Momma comin' to visit us, then you don't believe in nothin' no more."

It was terrible quiet for a while. Then Papa jest took the lantern and he left.

"I guess he's gone to the barn," said Alvin.

After a while, John Neal said, "We've still got Sandy Claws."

"We ain't still got anything," said Alvin.

"When Papa said there wouldn't be no Christmas, he meant ever'thing about Christmas."

"No," said Maude. "John Neal's right! Santa Claus comes ever year, and he don't know what Papa said. That means he is gonna come and leave . . ."

"A Christmas tree!" said John Neal. "Sandy Claws brings the Christmas tree. Christmas morning, we git up and there is the tree that Sandy Claws left."

"Then, we decorate the tree. That's what we did last year."

Alvin and Hannah Rose looked at one another, and they looked at me. In a way they are right. I mean, Papa can't tell Santa Claus what to do.

Hannah Rose said, "I say that we jest stay out of Papa's way, and keep quiet. Besides, there are presents that don't cost anything."

"We can make presents," said Maude.

"Or give things that belongs to us," said John Neal.

So, we went to bed, not knowing when Papa come in. And, somehow, we are going to have Christmas. I guess we are all worried about how we could do that without Papa knowing, but we will work it out. When I was almost asleep, Maude come in my room and shook me and pointed out the window. Up on Chilly Knob was Grammy's light. "I like seeing the light up there," said Maude. Me, too.

This morning, Papa was asleep in front of the fire,

with his pipe in his hand. He don't sleep in the bed now. Sometimes, he stands in front of the bedroom door like he was thinking about going in, but then don't. We never go in there either. The window shades are down, and it has a musty smell. I told Grammy about it, and she said, "Somebody should raise the window and let the sunshine in!"

THIS IS ABOUT MISS CALLOWAY. Miss Calloway come to see us today. She's the best teacher at Wide Awake, and she knows all of us, but she is my English teacher and she is very special to me. She said she heard that we wasn't coming back to school and she was upset. She stood there on the porch and talked to us.

"Do you miss school?" she said.

"Not me!" crowed Hannah Rose. "I'm having a good time jest doing what I want!"

"Me too," said Alvin.

Maude didn't say nothin'.

"I know you miss English, Becca," she said to me.
I nodded.

"All of this will work out somehow," she said.
"And you will be back in school after Christmas."

When she left, she asked me to walk a piece with
her. When we got below the house, she give me
this little package.

"This is a little something from me to you," she
said. "Don't wait until Christmas. You open it as
soon as you get back to the house."

Then, she looked real hard at me and said, "You
see and feel things, Becca. You describe them in
your writing, but there are other ways to describe
what you see and feel."

Then she smiled and she was gone.

I opened the little package on the porch. It was a water color set!

THIS IS WHAT HAPPENED TODAY AND TONIGHT. It is Christmas Eve today and this morning we decided that everthing would work out. Maude and John Neal found Momma's Christmas tree decorations. They was back up and under the eaves of the attic in a hidey-hole Momma had up there. They brung them down stairs and laid them all out on the table. Some of them Momma had baked from bread dough and painted, and some of them Papa had whittled. A few was store-bought, like the cornhusk Angel that goes on top of the tree. And John Neal thought the Angel looked like Momma, 'cause she had long goldie hair jest like the Angel. Alvin said that Momma didn't have no wings growing out of her back. John Neal said, he reckoned Momma had wings now, he bet, and on and on the argument went. Then Alvin said that the Angel was supposed to be the one that come to announce the birth of Jesus. That's when the trouble started.

"Who was Jesus' Momma and Papa?" said John Neal. He was asking Hannah Rose since, being the oldest, 'cept me, she was supposed to know.

"Well, Mary was the Momma and this man named Joseph was the Papa," said Alvin.

"No, the Holy Ghost was the Papa," said Hannah Rose. "Joseph didn't even know that Jesus was comin' till the Angel told him."

"But he was Mary's husband," said Alvin. "Anyway, forgit about that part. The important part is when they went to pay the taxes and they ended up in this town and couldn't find no place to stay, so they had to stay in a barn."

"And that's where Jesus was born," said Hannah Rose.

"In a barn," said Alvin.

"Like our barn?" said John Neal.

"I guess so," said Alvin.

"And the wise men come," said Hannah Rose.

"And the shepherds who was out watching their sheep," said Alvin.

"How did they know to come and see Jesus?" said John Neal.

"Because of a star," said Hannah Rose. "They followed a star."

"And they was Angels," said Alvin. "Don't forgit the Angels."

"Was there cows and sheep and animals and all like that in the barn?" said Maude.

"Oh, yes," said Alvin. "They got down on their knees and adored Jesus."

"The cows and the sheep did?" said John Neal.

"Yes," said Alvin.

"And the trees too," said Hannah Rose.

"Trees?" said John Neal.

"Yes, the trees come and got down on their knees and worshiped and adored Jesus," said Hannah Rose.

"How does a tree do that?" said Maude.

"Do what?" said Hannah Rose.

"Git down on its knees."

"Well," said Hannah Rose. "They got limbs."

"What kind of trees?" said John Neal.

"Oh, pines and cedars and spruce."

"That must've been a real big barn," said Maude. "I mean, if the cows and the horses and the sheep..."

"And the Angels," said John Neal. "Don't forgit the Angels!"

"And the wise men and the shepherds and all..."

"Did the Angels fly around or did they roost like our chickens do?" said John Neal.

"Angels don't roost, John Neal," said Maude, "They jest keep a' flyin' and a' flapin' around."

"They was flying around singing 'Hallalu-ya!'" said Hannah Rose.

"What was the Baby Jesus doin' while everbody was crowdin' in there?" said Maude.

"Oh, he was jest lyin' in his manger, wavin' his little arms around. He jest loved it," said

Hannah Rose.

Then Papa come home. There was the Christmas tree decorations all laid out on the table and he seen them right away. Alvin tried to explain.

"Papa, we know there won't be a Christmas, but we thought there might be a tree," he said.

"Since the tree is alwus brung by Santa Claus, and since he don't know we can't have Christmas this year..." said Hannah Rose —

"...he will bring the tree anyways," said Alvin.

"And so we thought it would be alright to go ahead and pull out the decorations."

Papa jest stared at us.

"And since Santa Claus don't know no better..." said Alvin —

"...he'll probably bring the tree," said Hannah Rose —

"...not knowing that we ain't having Christmas this year," said Alvin.

Papa stared at us some more. "So you think Santa Claus is coming," he said. We all nodded.

"Since he don't know what you decided," said Hannah Rose.

Papa went to the closet and got the shotgun. He loaded both barrels.

"It's gitten pretty dark out there," said Papa. "I guess Santa is flying around this holler by now." Then, he walked out the door. We heard both barrels go off behind the house.

Papa come back in and opened the shotgun. Two smoking hulls popped out in his hand.

"I don't know if I hit him or not," said Papa, "but I bet I scared him pretty bad. He won't be stopping here tonight! Now, git to bed."

And we went. That's where I am now, writing in

my book. Maude's cryin' herself to sleep worrying about Santa Claus, and this seems like the darkest, longest night of the year. When I looked out the window at Chilly Knob, Grammy's light was out.

Now it's a few hours later. Jest after I wrote that Grammy's light was out, I heard a little shuffling sound on the attic steps. So I got up real quiet out of the bed. From the top of the attic steps I could see John Neal tip-toeing down the last step. Then he begun tip-toeing around, putting each little foot down careful as he went, to where Papa was asleep in his chair in front of the fire. Papa's boots was setting by his chair and his legs was stretched out. John Neal creeped up to Papa and by the light from the fireplace, I seen that he had Fuzzy in his arms. He stopped jest afore he got to Papa's chair and begun to pat Fuzzy and whisper to him. He whispered so soft I could barely hear him. He said, "Fuzzy, you and me been friends a long, long time. Long as I can 'member. You're the goodest friend I have in the whole world. But Papa needs you now. You got to go an' be Papa's friend 'cause Papa is real sad. Be his friend. An' make him laugh like you make me laugh. And then Momma, an' Sandy Claws and all the Angels will come and everthing will be fine like it usta be. Now, you don't cry, jest go on and stay with Papa." Then, John Neal held up Fuzzy and kissed him on his nose. "Bye Fuzzy," he said.

Then he done this. He put Fuzzy down and very, very gentle-like he begun to pull off one of Papa's socks. Papa moved in his sleep and John Neal quick as anything scooted around and hid behind Papa's chair. Papa begun to snore again. John Neal come out from behind the chair and begun to pull at that sock till he had it peeled off Papa's foot. He picked up Fuzzy and commenced to stuff him into the sock 'till jest his head was peeking out the top. He give Fuzzy in the sock one last big hug, and laid him down in Papa's lap. An' without looking back, John Neal tip-toed back up the stairs.

I got out of sight afore John Neal could see me and waited till he got to sleep. Then I went and waked up the others and told them with my signing what John Neal had done. So, they all got their presents for Papa out from where they was hiding them and tiptoed down the stairs and put them in Papa's lap. Hannah Rose had made a match-holder so Papa would alwus have matches for his pipe. And there was a new set of guitar strings from Alvin. I jest knew he'd spent ever last penny he'd saved to buy hisself a juice harp like Papa's. Maude had took a apple and stuck it full of cloves and tied it around with a little ole piece of ribbon. She'd watched Momma make 'em lots of times to hang in our clothes closet to make it smell good in there. It must of took her a long time, with her little hands, to stick that apple 'round with cloves.

After they all crept back up to bed I knew it was time for me to finish my book, so I set down at

Papa

Papa at Christmas

the kitchen table, and now I am writing this. We love you, Papa. I'm going to stop now, and leave my present with the rest.

THIS IS ABOUT CHRISTMAS. I asked Papa to let me have the book back so I could write about this day and all that happened.

Jest when I got to the top of the steps on my way back to bed Papa woke up. He stretched and wiggled his toes and then he seen he only had one sock on. I heard him say, "What? Now I know I had two of 'em on." Then he looked down in his lap and seen all the presents. The first one he picked up was Fuzzy in his sock. He looked real puzzled, and he turned him around and around in his big ole hands. Then he pulled Fuzzy out of his sock, and he grinned. Next, this real low chuckle come out of him. Papa jest about laughed!

He put Fuzzy down gentle on his knee an' he talked to Fuzzy, like John Neal alwus does. Papa said, "I took that button off m'weddin' shirt an' give it to her. So's she could sew it on for yer nose." He set there awhile pettin' Fuzzy on his knee. An' then he begun to look at his other presents. He picked up the clove apple and the guitar strings and the match-holder one by one and looked at them real careful. The last one he picked up was my book. He took his finger and run it over Momma's cross-stitched roses all around the cover. Then he begun to read. His hand would shake ever'time he turned the page.

There come a tear slidin' down his cheek. Then my book fell in his lap and he covered his face up with his hands. He pitched his head down in his lap an' jest cried and cried.

When he quit, he pulled his hands off his face and jerked up straight. His eyes was jest wild. He stared around at ever'thing in the room like it was the first time he'd saw it. I thought I better git back to bed afore he looked up and seen me. Jest when I pulled the covers over my head I heard Papa say, "Oh my God, what have I done? What have I done to our children?"

I think Papa had a change of heart. And maybe reading my book and seeing ever'thing that had happened in one piece helped make a difference. But I know this for sure! Along about jest before daylight they was a sound downstairs that woke us all up.

"Ho, Ho, Hooo! Ho, Ho, Hoooooo!"

Then, we heard the door slam. When we got downstairs, there it was! The Christmas tree. John Neal run to the window and yelled, "I see him! There he goes! Sandy Claws!"

We all run over and looked. There was something out there. It was jumping and running from tree to tree, and then it was gone. Then, Alvin said, "Look at this!" There was a note on the Christmas tree. It said, "Santa Claus don't scare off that easy! Merry Christmas!" "He wasn't even afraid of Papa's twelve-gauge!" said Alvin. "He come and brung the tree anyways!"

Then, the backdoor opened and there was Papa.

"Alvin," he said, "Come here." Poor Alvin went. I don't know what he thought, but he looked worried. We all followed.

"What do you want, Papa?"

"What do I want?" Papa stared at us. Then, he smiled. "Why, I want you to help me git this yule log in the house. Come on, now, we have to hurry. It's almost daylight and it should be all fired up by now."

And they did that. It took some doing. They was

both sweating and breathing hard by the time it was resting in the fireplace where it took up almost all the room.

"Santa Claus come, even after you shot at him," said Alvin.

"Yep," said Papa. "I guess he showed me!" Papa laughed and clapped Alvin on the back. Alvin grinned. They stood there looking at the yule log.

"It has to burn for twelve days," said Alvin.

"I know," said Papa.

"We have to git Grammy afore we light the fire," said Alvin.

"I know," said Papa. "She's on her way now." Sure enough, Grammy walked in the door. She had something in a paper sack that she handed to Alvin. He reached in the sack and brung out a little chunk of wood.

"That's from last year's yule log," said Grammy.

"You alwus save a piece to start the next year's fire. That way, the fire jest goes on. In a way, it never is a new fire, 'cause you use the old log to start it. Sorta like us. When somebody dies, a part of them goes on, too."

Papa reached for his new match-holder on the fireboard, and with a little pile of pine shavings, he started the fire under the little charred chunk of wood. It blazed right up! Alvin added some pine kindling and in no time, it was really going.

"Thank you for my match-holder, Hannah Rose," said Papa.

"You're welcome," said Hannah Rose.

"How come it burns so good?" said Maude.

"It alwus does," said Grammy. "It's like it wants to burn."

"Is that little chunk of wood from your fireplace, Grammy?" said John Neal.

"No, John Neal, it was from yours. Your Momma saved it jest like I taught her. I jest knew where she kept it."

"You mean, we've alwus had a yule log?" said Alvin. "How come we didn't know 'bout it?"

"Well, the 'old fire' is something that the adults don't talk 'bout to the children. They jest do it. It's a part of Christmas that they keep to theirselves."

"But we know 'bout it this year!" said John Neal.

"That's right," said Grammy. "You know 'bout it this year, 'cause this Christmas is special." She looked at Papa.

Papa went into the kitchen and in a minute he come back out. He had Fuzzy peeking over his overalls bib, and he had Maude's clove-apple 'ahanging by the ribbon around his ear like it was a Christmas tree ornament. He looked so funny we all jest bust out laughing. And he had his guitar. It looked all shined and spiffy, and it had

Alvin's new strings. He set down in his big chair in front of the fireplace and he wiggled his eyebrows. Then, he bent over with his ear next to the sound hole and said, "What? What?" Then, he laughed and said, "Whoa!"

"What, Papa, what?" said John Neal.

"I think it's a new song," said Papa. He started picking the strings. "But the guitar said you had to help."

"Like we used to," said Maude.

"Yes, honey, like we used to," said Papa. "Now, what all you want in this here song? Call 'em out!"

"Angels flying around!" said John Neal.

"And 'bout the cows and horses kneeling down," said John Neal.

"Snow and fire and...a Christmas tree!" said Maude in a singsong voice.

"Whoa!" said Papa, "That's a big order! I jest don't know..."

"Come on, Papa, you can do it!" said Alvin.

Papa acted like he was real worried, but he started playing. Then, Maude said, "Put Momma in the song, too!"

There was a hitch in the song, like Papa had lost the melody for a minute. Then, he started playing again. "And Momma," he said. The guitar was making sounds like little bells tinkling. The music got bigger and Papa begun to sing.

Well, I was sleepin' last night
There was somethin' not right,
When an Angel of light said, "Ya missed it."
Well, you been pinin' so long
That it's done come and gone
An' ya can't sing no song about Christmas.

They is snow falling down,
They is cows kneeling down
An' they's Angels flyin' round
    when it's Christmas!
An' your Momma is nigh
With the fire burnin' high
And you cannot deny that it's Christmas!

And the Angel of Love is with you.
And the tree and presents, too;
And the heart of the fire
    when the Spirit is nigh...
Merry Christmas together with you!

An' then, Papa's music changed and it sounded like Momma's dulcimore. He got real surprised lookin', but he kept on strumming. Then he sung.

Love if you miss me
While we are apart,
I'll send you a Sign of Love
into your heart.

After, he shifted back to our Christmas made-up song and his guitar sounded like alwus.

And the Spirit of Love is with you,
And the joy and the mem'ry too;
And the heart of the fire
*   when the Spirit is nigh . . .*
I'm together forever with you . . .
We're Together Forever with you!

Then, Papa give his little nod for everbody to all join in.

I'm Together Forever with you.
Together Forever
We're Always Together
Together Forever with You!

Then John Neal said, "Momma's here!"

Nobody said nothin' for a while. We all looked at Papa. He said, "Yes, she is." He went over to the fireplace and knelt down like he was warming his hands. "Merry Christmas, Sharon!" he said. And Momma was there. We all knew it was true 'cause we felt it. All we had to do was look at each other and we knew Momma was there — had alwus been there.

"Merry Christmas, Momma!" said Maude. We all chimed in.

"Merry Christmas, Momma," I said in my heart.

All of a sudden Papa jumped up in front of the fire place and flung out his arms. He was grinnin' that ole grin of his that looked like the sun coming up. Then he reached out and pulled ever one of us into his arms in a big bear hug. And he was a laughin', with tears rollin' down from his eyes at the same time, and hugging and squeezin' us all tight and saying over and over again, "You're my Angels. You're Papa's Angels."

Papa's Songs

THE MAPLE TREE SONG.

Grins Jenkins

1. Red, gold and yellow leaves All fall on me   Blanket of
2. Springtime will come but while we are apart   I'll fold your

memories, Old Maple Tree. Summer has gone away All fall on me —
memory into my heart. Love, if you miss me while we are apart   I'll

Winter is calling you, Old Maple Tree. Winter is calling, so stoke up the
Send you a sign of love, into your heart. (go to 𝄋) End:

fire   Deep in the night may you warm us a while. Christmas is coming, so

stoke up the fire   Spirit of love may you warm us a while . [go to 𝄋]2.]

THE SIMPLE SIGNS OF LOVE

TOGETHER FOREVER

Grins Jenkins

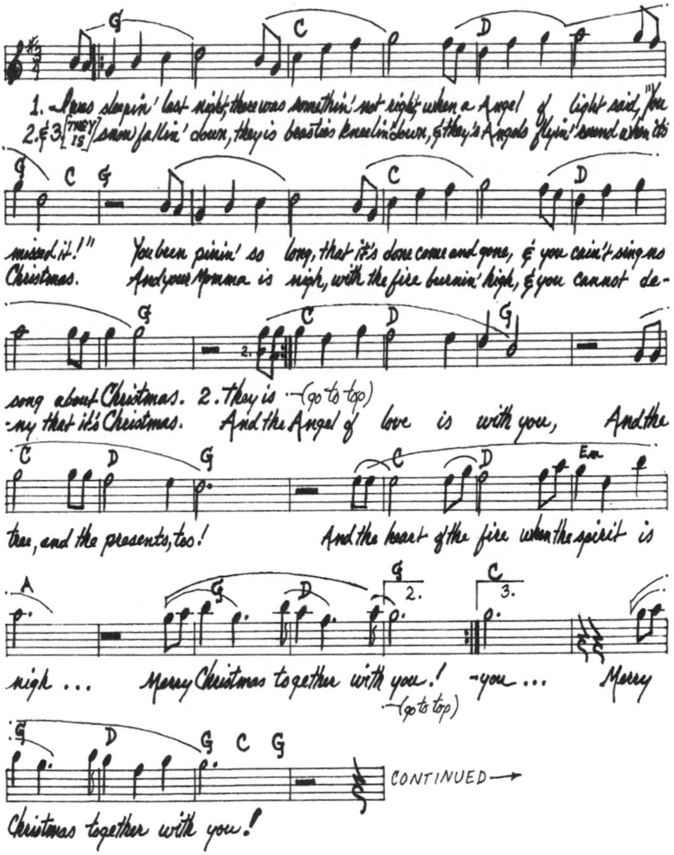

... Love, if you miss me while we are apart, I'll send you a

sign of love into your heart.

And the spirit of love is with you, And the joy, and the mem'ry

too — And the heart of the fire when the spirit is nigh — I'm to-

-gether forever with you... We're together forever with you!

(ECHO) →

Echo

I'm to-gether forever with you... Together forever – we're always to-gether, together for ever with you!

Acknowledgments

A THANK YOU from my heart to you beings, who with your unique, diverse gifts and abilities, have, over the last nine years, made joyful contributions to this little story. Beloved, for your love, your laughter, your magic, and your "Papa"; John Roman, for your songs that make our hearts sing; Elsa Sibley, for your beautiful pictures; Christina Howle, for your creation of the quintessential "Fuzzy"; brother Rex Reed, for your nurturing of the story; sister Gaylan "Nanny I" Wilson, for your unflagging enthusiasm and tireless typing; sister Dr. Gay Dawn Claiborne, for your everloving rereading; Cuz Jean Snyder, for your angelic support; Clarinda Ross (TD), for your love and direction of the play; John Michel, for your expert and generous assistance with rewrites; David Thomas, for your productions at the A.R.T. Station; all the casts of wonderful children and Papas, for acting in the play; Susan Clark and Alex Karris, for your friendship and belief; Jan Davidson, for your mountain voice; Ran Shaffner, for your inspiring critique; Miss Calloway, for your faith; Arthur Hancock, for your songs of 1987; Phyllis Rab, for your being there; Terry Kay, for your most excellent suggestion; Marc Allen, for your Visionary Business and your exquisite editing; Becky "Nanny II" Benenate, for Momma's roses; Munro Magruder, for your dancin' the story out there; Aaron Kenedi, for your amazing text. Harry Hart-Browne (P.P.), for your notes of love; Thomas Meyer, for your Enlightened Composition of Being; Jackie and Teddy Wilcox, for your being.

And most especially thank you to all the angels, for your inspirational wonder and for hovering around.

— C.W.P.

About the Authors

COLLIN WILCOX PAXTON is best known for her film portrayal of Mayella Violet Ewell in the classic movie *To Kill a Mockingbird*. Her first Broadway play, in 1958, won her the Clarence Derwent Award for Best Supporting Actress On or Off Broadway that year. Since that time, she has appeared on stage in New York, London, and Los Angeles, and been in eighty television shows and fifteen films. Her play, *Papa's Angels*, has had three successful stage productions. Collin, her husband Scott, and their exaltation of animals live in the old log family farmhouse where she was raised in Highlands, North Carolina.

GARY CARDEN, storyteller, lecturer, and playwright, has coauthored two other books, *Belled Buzzards, Hucksters and Grieving Spectres: Strange and True Tales of the Appalachian Mountains;* and *From the Brothers Grimm.* In addition, he contributed a chapter on the mythology of the Southeastern Tribes for *Native American Myth and Legend* published by Salamander Press in London. Carden's play *The Raindrop Waltz* will be published by Palmetto Script Press in the fall of 1996. Carden's video *Blow the Tannery Whistle!* has been aired on PBS. Carden lives in his grandfather's house in Sylva, North Carolina, with three cats and his dog Teddie.

ABOUT THE ARTIST

ELSA ALEXANDRA SIBLEY, artist and equestrienne, paints portraits in her Atlanta studio and paints landscapes in Highlands, North Carolina, inspired by the mountains through which she rides. Her watercolors for *Papa's Angels* are her first venture in book illustration. She lives with her companion, Jim, and her two horses in Atlanta, Georgia.

About the Songwriter

JOHN ROMAN has been a musician for thirty years. He is an expert songwriter and experienced guitarist. The National Academy of Songwriters named him The Songwriter of the Year (1995). John Roman's songs, like traditions, speak the truth, give hope to the soul, and capture the heart of Appalachia. He lives with his wife, Trace, and their son Cai, in a turn-of-the-century barn that he renovated in Highlands, North Carolina.

New World Library is dedicated to
publishing books and cassettes that inspire
and challenge us to improve the quality of
our lives and our world.

For a catalog of our fine books and
cassettes contact:

New World Library
14 Pamaron Way
Novato, CA 94949
Phone: (415) 884-2100
FAX: (415) 884-2199

Or call toll free:
(800) 227-3900

Blessings